E F MOO

D0356671

SNOW FUN

CARTOON NETWORK®

by E. S. Mooney #9108
Based on
"THE POWERPUFF GIRLS,"
as created by Craig McCracken

Vineyard Christian School

1011 East Ave. I

Lancaster, CA 93535

SCHOLASTIC INC.

New York   Toronto   London   Auckland   Sydney
Mexico City   New Delhi   Hong Kong   Buenos Aires

ISBN 0-439-44224-9

Cover and interior illustrations by the Thompson Brothers

Designed by Peter Koblish

12 11 10 9 8 7 6 5 4 3 2 1   2 3 4 5 6 7/0

Printed in the U.S.A.
First printing, December 2002

Chapter 1

*The city of Townsville! A city of delight-
ful distractions, pleasurable pastimes, and
amusing amusements! A city of fun and fes-
tivity! A city of thrills! A city with . . . what's
this? Three annoyed, fed up, bored little su-
perheroes? Why, Powerpuff Girls? What's
wrong?*

"I'm bored!" Buttercup complained
for the hundredth time that Saturday.

"We could do our 6,000-piece Eiffel
Tower puzzle," Blossom suggested.

"No way!" Buttercup replied.

"No more puzzles!" Bubbles agreed.

"Well, I guess we already did our 6,000-piece Statue of Liberty puzzle," Blossom said.

"You mean our 5,999-piece Statue of Liberty puzzle," Buttercup corrected.

"It would have been a lot prettier if we'd been able to put the torch in her hand," Bubbles agreed. "Hey, wanna look around some more for that piece?"

"No!" Blossom and Buttercup said together.

The Girls sat silently for a moment.

"We could play *Alien Invader* on the computer again," Buttercup said.

"No way," Blossom said. "You only want to play if we let you be the Alien Invader."

"Yeah, and then you just want to de-

stroy all us Earthlings," Bubbles added. "And that's not very nice."

"Bubbles, that's the point of the game," Buttercup said.

"It's still not nice," Bubbles pointed out.

The Girls sat in silence again.

Professor Utonium came into the

room. He held a feather duster in his hand.

"Hello, Girls," the Professor said cheerfully. "What are you up to this fine Saturday?"

"Nothing," Buttercup grumbled.

"We're bored," Blossom complained.

"We have nothing to do," Bubbles added.

"Well," the Professor began, "let me think. How about reading a book?"

"Read 'em all already," Blossom said.

"A board game?" the Professor suggested.

"Played 'em," Bubbles said.

"TV?"

"Nothing on," Buttercup said.

Bubbles gazed out the window. "You

4

know what I wish?" she said. "I wish it would snow."

"Then we could go sledding!" Blossom said.

"And make snow angels!" Bubbles added.

"And have snowball fights!" Buttercup said eagerly.

The Professor chuckled and shook his head. "Well, Girls, if it's snow you want, I'm afraid you'll just have to wait. I'm sorry, but there's no snow in the forecast."

The three Girls stared out the window and sighed.

"That stinks," Buttercup said.

"I know," Bubbles said suddenly. "Let's use pretend power!"

"Huh?" Blossom and Buttercup said, looking at her.

"You know!" Bubbles said. "Like they say on *TV Puppet Pals* — 'To get your wish this very hour, just use a little pretend power!'" *The TV Puppet Pals* was Bubbles's favorite show.

"You mean we're supposed to *pretend* it's snowing?" Blossom said.

Bubbles nodded.

"That's dumb!" Buttercup said.

"Come on, let's go outside and give it a try," Bubbles said.

"I guess we don't have anything better to do," Blossom said with a shrug.

"Oh, all right," Buttercup said. "But I still say it's dumb."

The Girls bundled up in their warmest winter things. Then they went outside.

Just look at those three Girls go! Look at them building imaginary snowmen! See how they roll around making grass-angels! Look, now they're having a dirt-ball fight! And building a fort out of rocks!

Finally, the Girls dragged out their sled and put it at the top of the highest hill in the neighborhood. They all climbed on the sled together.

"Wheee!!!" Bubbles yelled with delight.

"Bubbles," Buttercup said, "this is really stupid."

"We're not even moving," Blossom pointed out. She got up off the sled, which was still sitting firmly in the grass at the top of the hill.

Buttercup stood up and brushed the grass off her coat. "None of this is any fun. I'm going inside."

"Me, too," Blossom said.

"I guess you guys are right," Bubbles said sadly. "I guess there are some wishes even pretend power can't take care of." Bubbles shrugged and followed her sisters.

When the Girls got into the house, they kicked off their dirty boots and shrugged off their grass-stained jackets.

"How was it, Girls?" the Professor asked eagerly. "Did you have fun?"

"No," Buttercup said.

"It was more fun sitting inside and staring out the window," Blossom answered.

"Pretend snow isn't anywhere near as

good as real snow," Bubbles told him dejectedly.

The Professor gazed at his Girls as they floated sadly down the hall. His Girls meant everything to him. If only there was something he could do to cheer them up.

Chapter 2

Later that night! Our three little super-heroes have finally come to the end of their dull, dreary day and are tucked in snug for the night. Or are they? Wait a minute! Bubbles is awake!

Bubbles turned over in bed. Her sisters were sound asleep beside her. Bubbles felt her stomach rumble.

Bubbles thought about how yummy a glass of milk would be. But she was scared to go downstairs by herself. It was the middle of the night. Even the Professor would be asleep now. What if giant spiders crawled out from under the bed and tried to grab her legs? What if a monster jumped out of the hall closet? What if a swarm of flying lizards attacked her on the stairs?

Bubbles nudged Blossom, who was lying beside her. She knew she would feel better if Blossom went with her.

"Blossom?" Bubbles whispered.

But Blossom was sound asleep. She didn't budge. Bubbles leaned over to peer at Buttercup in the dark. Maybe she could ask Buttercup to go with her. But Bubbles knew that Buttercup would just make fun of her for being afraid.

Bubbles's stomach growled again. She thought of the nice carton of milk downstairs in the refrigerator. Maybe if she flew as fast as she could, she wouldn't notice how dark it was.

Bubbles took a deep breath and zoomed out from under the covers. She flew out of the room and down the stairs.

But to Bubbles's surprise, the house wasn't completely dark after all. A light was coming from inside the Professor's laboratory.

Bubbles flew over to the laboratory door. She could hear the Professor working inside. Bubbles hovered in the doorway.

The Professor was so busy with what he was doing that he didn't even notice Bubbles.

In front of him on his worktable were lots of tubes and tools. The

Professor was working on screwing something into a large silver box in front of him. The box had several dials and buttons on it.

Bubbles was just about to ask the Professor what he was doing when he began muttering to himself.

"Now if I can just tighten this valve here," the Professor said, still working with his screwdriver, "that will increase the atmospheric pressure inside the barometric vaporizer enough to crystallize the liquid into perfect fluffy white flakes of snow."

Bubbles gasped. Snow! Did the Professor say something about snow?

"Perfect!" the Professor said, putting down his screwdriver. "My invention is complete. I'll just pour in the special snow formula, aim the snowblower tube out the window, and set the timer for five A.M. That

way there will be plenty of snow on the ground for my Girls when they wake up in the morning." The Professor smiled with satisfaction. "Won't they be surprised!"

Bubbles could hardly believe what she had heard. The Professor had invented a snowmaking machine, just for her and her sisters. He was the best Professor anyone could ever have. Bubbles wanted to run into the lab and throw her arms around him.

But then she thought a moment. The Professor had said he wanted to surprise the Girls. Maybe Bubbles shouldn't ruin the surprise by letting the Professor know what she had seen. Quietly, Bubbles floated away from the lab. She headed for the kitchen to get herself a glass of milk.

By the time Bubbles finished drinking her glass of milk, she was so excited about the snowmaker that she could hardly keep still. She and her sisters were going to have so much fun tomorrow! Just wait until Blossom and Buttercup saw the surprise!

On her way back from the kitchen, Bubbles decided to take one last peek at what the Professor was doing. But when she stopped by the lab, the lights were out.

The Professor had stopped work for the night and gone to bed at last.

Cautiously, Bubbles flipped on the light in the lab. She just wanted one more look at that pretty silver snowmaker.

Bubbles floated over to the snowmaker and gazed at it. She and Blossom and Buttercup were going to have so much fun tomorrow. Bubbles really appreciated what the Professor was doing for them. She wished she could do something nice for him, too.

Then Bubbles had an idea. Maybe she could make the snow machine into a super-duper snow machine!

Bubbles eyed the container of Chemi-

cal X on the shelf just above her. After all, Chemical X was what had made Bubbles and her sisters so special, right?

Bubbles thought a moment. Maybe she could help the Professor by adding just a drop of Chemical X to his snow formula. That would probably make the snow super-duper fun!

Oh, no, Bubbles! What are you doing?

Bubbles flew up to the shelf and grabbed the container. She opened the special compartment on the snowmaker where she'd seen the Professor pour in the snow formula.

"There!" she said, adding a drop of Chemical X. "Now this snow will be the bestest snow ever!"

Bubbles flew back to her room, filled with excitement. Just wait till Blossom and Buttercup saw how fantastic the special snow was! And then Bubbles could tell them that she was the one who made it so great! The Professor would be so thankful for her help, and everyone would really appreciate what she had done!

What a great idea!

Chapter 3

The next morning! Just look at that snow! Why, there's a beautiful, glistening white blanket covering everything! And it's still coming down!

The moment Bubbles opened her eyes, she popped out of bed and zoomed over to the window.

"Snow!" she yelled. "Snow! Snow!"

Blossom and Buttercup were at her side in a second.

"All right!" Buttercup yelled.

"Let's go outside!" Blossom said.

The Girls dressed with superspeed. They zoomed into their warmest clothes and their waterproof boots. As they flew down the stairs they passed the Professor.

"Why, hello, Girls," the Professor said. "How do you like the —"

"Can't talk now, Professor," Buttercup cut him off.

"It's snowing!" Blossom added, zooming off after her sister.

Bubbles paused on the stairs to smile at the Professor. "We all love the snow, Professor," she said sweetly. "It's super!" Then she flew off after her sisters.

"Watch out, Bubbles!" Buttercup yelled as Bubbles flew outside. She lobbed a snowball right at her sister.

Bubbles ducked out of the way, and the snowball went whizzing over her head.

"Ha-ha! You missed me!" Bubbles said, giggling. She scooped up some snow of her own.

But then Bubbles heard a smashing sound behind her. The windshield of a nearby parked car was shattered.

Blossom zoomed over to the car. "Buttercup, did you do this?"

Buttercup shrugged. "Oops. I didn't think I threw it that hard."

"Watch out for this one!" Bubbles giggled. She threw her snowball at Buttercup. But the snowball missed Buttercup and hit the corner of a house instead. To Bubbles's amazement, the corner of the house was completely shattered, and bricks flew out in all directions.

"Bubbles!" Blossom scolded. "Buttercup! You know you can't use superpowers for stuff like this! You're going to destroy the whole neighborhood. Do it like this."

Blossom made a snowball and tossed it at Buttercup. But as the snowball flew through the air, it started gathering speed. Soon, it was zooming

through the air, leaving a white trail behind it. Finally, it smashed into Buttercup's stomach, sending her flying.

Buttercup landed against a fence, making a big hole in it. She got back to her feet, her green eyes sparking with anger.

"Oh, yeah?" she said angrily to Blossom. "You mean like *this*?"

Buttercup lobbed a snowball back at Blossom. This one hit Blossom in the shoulder, sending her into a superspin that dug a deep hole into the ground.

"Wait! Stop!" Blossom cried, climbing back out of the hole. "There's something wrong with these snowballs!"

"Hey, look!" Bubbles said, pointing to a group of kids across the street. "It looks like they're going to have a snowball fight, too!"

The kids had separated into two groups. Each group was building up a pile of snowballs to use as ammunition.

"Oh, no!" Blossom said. "We've got to stop them before someone gets hurt!"

The Girls zoomed across the street.

"Stop!" Blossom called to the kids. "Don't throw any of those snowballs!"

"Don't listen to them!" a boy yelled. "It's a trick! They probably just want to ambush us with their own snow-balls!"

"No, really!" Bubbles called. "We mean it. We —"

She was silenced by a snowball that came hurling toward her. The snowball hit Bub-bles with such force that she was thrown high into the air.

"Wow!" one of the kids said to another as Bubbles landed in the snow. "You just creamed one of The Powerpuff Girls."

Within seconds, snowballs were flying in

all directions. The Girls zoomed into action.

A snowball was superspeeding toward a little girl. Bubbles swooped down and grabbed the girl, taking her out of the snowball's path just in time. Another snowball smashed into a tree trunk, shattering it and sending an explosion of wood into the air. Buttercup darted up and zoomed around, catching the wood pieces before they could hit anyone. Blossom zigzagged through the air, trying to knock the snowballs off course so no one would get hurt.

Finally, the Girls stopped the fight. Several houses had been damaged by the snowballs, and there were large craters all over the ground. Most of the children were crying.

The Girls told the children to go home. Then they headed back toward home themselves. They were exhausted.

"This snow is weird," Buttercup said, kicking at some of the snow with her boot.

"It's almost like it has some kind of superpower," Blossom agreed.

Bubbles didn't say anything. She was starting to think about something — something she didn't want to think about.

Bubbles tried to push the bad thought out of her mind. She flopped down in the snow. "I think it's the bestest snow ever!" she insisted. She lay on her back and moved her arms and legs, making a snow angel. "See?"

Bubbles made another angel, and another. Soon she had a whole row of angels.

"Come on, Bubbles, let's go inside," Blossom said.

The Girls trooped into the house.

"Hello, Girls," the Professor sang out cheerfully. "I hope you had fun in the snow." He smiled at them. "You know I made it especially for you."

"*Made* it?" Blossom asked.

"What do you mean?" Buttercup said.

The Professor chuckled. "Oh, just a little invention I came up with. I knew you Girls were really wishing for snow. So I invented a special snowmaker and set it to start snowing early this morning."

"Isn't he the bestest Professor ever?" Bubbles exclaimed.

"Well . . ." Blossom began.

"What is it?" the Professor asked. "Don't you like the snow? I thought you Girls loved snow."

"We do," Buttercup said. "But this is snow with a major attitude."

"The snowballs seem to pack a little too much punch," Blossom explained.

"Too much punch, eh?" the Professor said. "Well, it's probably just a little glitch. Don't worry about it, Girls. A couple of small adjustments to the machine and the snow will be just perfect. You'll see. Now, how about some hot chocolate and muffins?"

But Bubbles was worried. The thought she had tried to push away was coming back. Bubbles tried to think about something else instead. She thought about rainbows and flowers, trying to push the bad thought out of her mind.

The Professor brought out three mugs of hot chocolate and a plate of muffins. The Girls sat down eagerly for breakfast.

But suddenly, there were screams outside.

Blossom zoomed over to the window. "Oh, no!" she said.

Bubbles and Buttercup flew over to look out of the window. Outside, hundreds of icicles were dropping off of buildings and traffic lights. But instead of falling to the ground, they were shooting through the air like ice-missiles, chasing people down the snowy streets. People screamed as they ran from the sharp ice-daggers.

"Looks like breakfast is gonna have to wait!" Blossom said as the Girls zoomed for the door.

Go, Girls, go!

Chapter 4

The Girls flew outside. The ice-missiles were slicing through the air.

"Help! Help!" a woman cried, running by, pushing a baby carriage.

"The ice! It's after us!" a man yelled as a pointy icicle chased him down the street.

Bubbles flew up into the air. She zoomed in front of one of the flying icicles and grabbed it. "Ooooh!" she yelled. "That's cold!"

The icicle was still speeding with incredible force, dragging Bubbles along with it. Bubbles used every ounce of strength she had. Finally, she managed to drag the icicle down toward the ground, sticking its sharp point into a tree trunk.

Bubbles looked up. Blossom and Buttercup were wrestling with icicles, too, trying to pull them down out of the sky. But there were so many of them! Bubbles zoomed back up to help her sisters.

The Girls zigzagged through the sky, pulling down the spears of ice. Finally, they were finished. There wasn't a single icicle left anywhere.

The Girls collapsed, panting, on a snowbank. A snowball went rolling by them on the ground, growing larger as it rolled.

"What is it with this snow?" Buttercup said.

"I don't know." Blossom shook her head. "It's almost like it's as strong as we are."

Bubbles didn't say anything. The thought she didn't want to think was coming back again. Bubbles hummed a pretty tune to keep her mind off it.

Suddenly, a dark shadow passed through the sky. The Girls looked up. A large, shadowy figure with wings was flying over them.

"W-what's that?" Bubbles asked, afraid.

Buttercup stared. "Beats me."

Blossom studied the figure as it flew back and forth above them. "You're not going to believe this," she said. "But I think that's one of your snow angels, Bubbles!"

"Really?" Bubbles said. She wasn't scared anymore. This was exciting.

"Look, there's another," Buttercup said. "And another."

A squadron of angel-shaped figures was gliding through the sky above them. As the Girls watched, one of the angels swooped down toward a nearby house. With the flip of a wing, the angel smashed a large window in the house and then soared back up into the sky.

"What the —" Buttercup said.

Suddenly, another angel swooped down, knocking over a nearby mailbox.

Two more angels soared down and turned over a car.

"Those snow angels are no angels!" Blossom cried. "They're more like snow *devils*! Come on, Girls!"

The Girls were already worn out from fighting the vicious icicles, but they zoomed into action to take on the nasty angels. Blossom soared up into the sky and socked one of the angels with a superpowered punch. But to her amazement, the angel barely even budged. Then it powered up and punched Blossom back.

Blossom was shocked. She wasn't

used to being punched back. She went on the attack again, with a series of rapid-fire punches and kicks. It took everything Blossom had, but finally the snow angel fell from the sky. It landed below on the ground in a crumpled heap.

Nearby, Bubbles and Buttercup were struggling to fight more angels. This wasn't an easy battle for any of The Powerpuff Girls.

Meanwhile, below them on the ground, the rolling snowball passed by again. It had gathered even more snow and grown even larger. Now it was crushing trees and cars in its path, and it was headed toward downtown Townsville.

Finally, the Girls defeated the last of the snow angels. They were exhausted. All they wanted to do was rest.

"Oh, no! Look!" Bubbles said. "The Powerpuff signal."

The heart-shaped beam of light flashed above them in the sky. The Mayor used the signal to let the Girls know when they were needed to protect Townsville.

"Something's going on downtown," Blossom said. "It must be that giant snowball. Come on, Girls!"

Go, Girls, go! Get that evil snow!

But when the Girls arrived in downtown Townsville, they were shocked to see that the snowball wasn't the only problem. An army of evil-looking snowmen

was marching down Main Street, their carrot noses pointed straight ahead of them.

A troop of snowmen marched into the police station.

"All right, freeze!" they yelled at the police.

Their leader, a snowman with a big snow-belly, threw the chief of police out into a snowbank. Then the snow-chief took the police chief's place behind the desk in the station.

One troop of snowmen marched into the bank and took over there. Another squadron took over the hospital. There were snowmen taking control of the supermarket, the newspaper office — even the Mr. Freezy ice-cream truck.

"We gotta fight 'em!" Buttercup yelled.

"How?" Blossom said. "There are thousands of them."

"But we're The Powerpuff Girls, right?" Bubbles piped up hopefully.

"Sure, but we could barely lick those snow angels," Blossom pointed out. "And getting those icicles and snowballs under control was really hard. How are we gonna fight an army of thousands of snowmen?"

"You're right, Blossom," Buttercup admitted reluctantly. "This snow seems to have some kind of special power."

Bubbles felt that yucky thought coming back to her again — the thought she'd been trying not to think. The thought was really trying to come this time, pushing its way into her brain. Bubbles decided to sing a song to try to keep the thought out of her head.

"Oh, old man winter is a jolly ole guy,

He makes the white stuff fall from the sky,

So bring out your skates and bring out your sled,

Till the wind blows cold and your cheeks turn red!"

"Bubbles, be quiet!" Buttercup yelled.

"This is no time to sing," Blossom agreed. "We have to figure out what to do."

Hurry, Girls! Before Townsville is completely snowed under!

43

"There's only one thing to do," Blossom decided. "We have to go home and talk to the Professor. After all, he's the one who started this whole thing."

"No he didn't!" Bubbles blurted. "I mean, no we don't!"

"Blossom's got it right," Buttercup said. "It was the Professor's invention that made all this evil snow. Maybe he can figure out a way to stop it."

"But, but —" Bubbles really didn't

want to go talk to the Professor about this. Besides, that bad thought she was having was coming around again. "Maybe we should check with the Mayor!" Bubbles said suddenly. "Maybe he's got an idea!"

"The *Mayor*?!" Blossom and Buttercup said together.

No one said anything.

"Well, we should probably check in at City Hall on our way home, just to make sure the Mayor's okay," Blossom said finally.

The Girls flew above the snow-covered city. The citizens of Townsville were nowhere to be seen. Everyone was hiding indoors. Meanwhile, the snowman army patrolled the streets, and the giant snowball continued rolling through town, growing bigger and bigger, and crushing everything in its path.

The Girls flew to City Hall. Snowmen stood guarding the entrance below. The Girls flew silently above them and zoomed through the Mayor's office window.

"Oh, no!" Bubbles gasped.

The Mayor and his assistant, Ms. Bellum, were frozen inside enormous blocks of ice.

"Poor Mayor! Poor Ms. Bellum!" Bubbles gasped.

"Come on, we can take them with us," Blossom said. "Maybe the Professor can think of a way to thaw them."

The Girls grabbed the two giant blocks of ice with the Mayor and Ms. Bellum inside. They flew out the window and headed for home.

Below them, the Girls could see the

evil snowmen building more snowmen to add to their army. They flew faster.

At home, the Girls put the giant blocks of ice containing the Mayor and Ms. Bellum down in the front hall.

"Professor!" Blossom called out. "Professor, where are you?"

"In here, Girls!" the Professor called.

The Girls found the Professor sitting in his favorite chair in the den. His feet were up on a footstool, and he had a large book open on his lap. A cup of hot tea sat on the table beside him.

"Oh, hello, Girls," the Professor said with a smile. "I was just catching up on some of my reading." He chuckled and closed the book. "There's nothing like a nice, cozy day inside with a book and a beautiful snowfall outside."

"Uh, that's what we wanted to talk to you about, Professor," Blossom said. "You see, there's a big problem with the snow you made."

The Professor frowned. "Girls, I'm very disappointed in your attitude. I went to a lot of trouble to make that snow machine for you so you could have fun today. Now, maybe the snow's not absolutely perfect, but —"

"Not perfect?!" Buttercup yelled. "It's destroying all of Townsville!"

"Professor, there's

49

something really wrong with the snow," Blossom said. "There are fierce icicles chasing people down, and snowballs are exploding things like bombs, and an army of evil snowmen has taken over the city!"

"But other than that stuff, it's really nice snow," Bubbles added.

The Professor put his hands to his head. "I can't believe it!" he said. "How could this have happened? I was only trying to invent something nice, something for you Girls to enjoy! How could it have gone so horribly wrong?! How could —"

Suddenly, the Professor was cut off by an enormous rumble from somewhere outside.

Oh, no! What now? Help, Girls, help!

chapter 6

"W-what was that?" Bubbles stammered.

The rumble was growing louder.

"We'd better go check it out!" Buttercup said.

The Girls flew outside. A tremendous wave of snow was rolling straight toward them.

"It's an avalanche!" Blossom cried. "Watch out!"

The wall of snow was practically on top

of them. Quickly, the Girls zoomed straight up into the sky. The avalanche crashed beneath them.

The Girls looked down at their house. It was completely covered in a huge mound of snow.

"Oh, no!" Bubbles gasped.

"The Professor!" Buttercup yelled.

"We've got to get him out!" Blossom cried.

The Girls swooped down and began digging with superspeed.

"We'll never get anywhere like this," Blossom said. "The snow is too thick! Use your eye beams!"

The Girls focused their eye beams on the snow. But even their laser-strong eye beams had no effect. The snow was solid.

"What is it with this snow?!" Butter-

cup yelled in frustration, still aiming her eye beams at the avalanche.

"It's almost like it has superpowers or something!" Blossom agreed, focusing her eye beams harder.

Suddenly, the bad thought that Bubbles had been trying not to think came flooding into her mind. What if the superpowered

snow was her fault? She might be respon-
sible for creating this horrible avalanche,
putting Townsville in danger, and making
the Professor feel really, really bad about
his invention!

Bubbles's head felt like it was about to
burst with the thought. She had to let it out.

"I put Chemical X in the snowmaker!"
she blurted out to her sisters.

"What?!" Blossom and Buttercup said together.

"I was only trying to help and make the snow super-duper fun and make everyone really happy and make the Professor feel proud!" Bubbles said.

"Bubbles, how could you?!" Blossom said. "You know we're not supposed to touch stuff in the Professor's lab!"

"Now you've ruined everything!" Buttercup screamed.

Bubbles felt her eyes welling up with tears. She felt so bad.

Bubbles had never cried while using her eye beams before. As the tears spilled out, they felt hot. That made Bubbles cry more.

"Stop crying, you baby!" Buttercup yelled.

"No, wait! Don't stop!" Blossom said. "Your tears are melting the snow, Bubbles!"

"Huh?" Bubbles said. She looked at the melted path her superhot tears had created in the snow. She smiled.

"I said, keep crying!" Blossom ordered.

"But now I don't feel sad anymore," Bubbles said, smiling. " 'Cause now the snow's melting."

"Well, you oughtta feel sad!" Buttercup yelled at her. "You practically destroyed Townsville with your dumb idea!"

Bubbles started to cry again.

"That's good," Blossom said. "Keep crying, Bubbles."

Soon, all the snow around the house was melted. The Girls zoomed off downtown, with Bubbles sniffling.

They hovered above the army of snowmen in the street.

"Okay, Bubbles," Blossom said. "Go ahead."

Bubbles turned on her eye beams. Then she shrugged. "I can't make any more tears."

"You dumb baby, you ruined the Professor's invention!" Buttercup yelled.

Bubbles started to cry again. Her laser-hot tears rained down on the snow army, melting them into a swirling river of water.

The Girls chased down the giant snowball. Bubbles turned on her eye beams.

"I bet the Professor will never forgive you!" Buttercup yelled at her.

Bubbles started to cry again. Soon the snowball was a giant puddle.

Water from melted snow was swirling through the streets of Townsville, carrying people along in the tide. The Girls swooped down and rescued people from the flood before flying back home.

In the front hall, the Professor was aiming a blow-dryer at the Mayor and Ms.

Bellum, who were still stuck in their blocks of ice.

"It's no use," the Professor said. "They're frozen solid. It seems like nothing can melt this ice."

"I'll take care of it, Professor," Bubbles said. She turned her eye beams on the blocks of ice. "After all," she added, "it's my fault that all this happened in the first place."

"What do you mean, Bubbles?" the Professor asked.

"I put Chemical X in the snowmaker, Professor," Bubbles confessed. She felt her eyes filling up with tears. "I know it was a bad thing to do, but I was only trying to help. And I'm really, really, really, really sorry!" Bubbles began to sob.

Bubbles's hot tears melted the blocks of ice.

"Phew!" the Mayor said, shaking himself off. "Chilly weather we're having lately. Damp, too."

"Thank you, Powerpuff Girls," Ms. Bellum said.

The Professor knelt down and looked firmly at Bubbles. "Bubbles, I hope you never, ever do anything like that again."

Bubbles sniffed. "I won't, Professor. I'm sorry."

"All right, then," the Professor said. "Now, how about some hot chocolate for everyone?"

And so, once again —

"Hey, look!" Bubbles shouted happily. She ran to the window to look outside. A few small white flakes were drifting down from the sky. "It's snowing!"

Her sisters groaned.

"Anybody for a puzzle?" Blossom asked. "I feel like staying in today."

"Me, too," Buttercup agreed.

And so, once again, the day is saved, thanks to The Powerpuff Girls!